Oliver Has Something to Say!

written by
Pamela Edwards

illustrated by
Louis Pilon

Lobster Press ™

Published by Lobster Press™
1620 Sherbrooke Street West, Suites C & D
Montréal, Québec   H3H 1C9
Tel. (514) 904-1100 • Fax (514) 904-1101
www.lobsterpress.com

Publisher: Alison Fripp
Editors: Alison Fripp & Meghan Nolan
Editorial Assistant: Katie Scott
Graphic Design & Production: Tammy Desnoyers

We acknowledge the financial support of the Government of Canada through the
Book Publishing Industry Development Program (BPIDP) for our publishing activities.

We acknowledge the support of the Canada
Council for the Arts for our publishing program.

We acknowledge the support of the government of Québec,
tax credit for book publishing, administered by SODEC.

Library and Archives Canada Cataloguing in Publication

Edwards, Pamela, 1948-
      Oliver has something to say! / Pamela Edwards; illustrations by Louis Pilon.

For ages 3-6.

ISBN-13: 978-1-897073-52-0 (bound)
ISBN-10: 1-897073-52-6 (bound)

      1. Picture books for children. I. Pilon, Louis, 1961- II. Title.

PS8609.D86O54 2007   jC813'.6   C2006-903963-1

Printed and bound in Canada.

For Bob, Ian, Tory,
and Mum and Dad,
with love.

– *Pamela Edwards*

To all of the people who
will enjoy this book.

– *Louis Pilon*

"Oliver, dear, would you like some more spaghetti?" asked his mom at the dinner table.

Oliver opened his mouth and his big sister, Margaret, said, "No, he doesn't want any more. He's got sauce all over his face and noodles in his hair."

Oliver closed his mouth.

"You're right," said Mom.
She looked at Oliver.

"Go wash your face, dear.
I'll deal with your hair later."

Oliver looked down at his plate.
A noodle fell out of his hair
and landed there.

The next day, it was Oliver's birthday party.

When it was time for the birthday cake, Azim's mom smiled at Oliver and asked, "How old are you today?"

Oliver opened his mouth and his dad said, "Four years old! He starts prekindergarten tomorrow!"

Oliver closed his mouth and stared at the candles on his cake.

Mom said, "Time to make a wish and blow out the candles, dear."

Oliver opened his mouth and Margaret blew them out.

Oliver closed his mouth and his friend Paul yelled, "What did you wish for, Ollie?"

Oliver opened his mouth and Mom said, "He wished for a train set. Oliver just LOVES trains. Close your mouth, dear."

When the party was over, Oliver stood by the door as the guests left. He heard Paul's mom whisper to Azim's mom,

"I wonder why Oliver doesn't say anything. He should be able to talk. Do you think he's shy?"

Azim's mom looked toward Oliver and said, "Yes, I think he is."

Oliver opened his mouth and Paul's mom shut the door.

He closed his mouth and opened the door.

Oliver opened his mouth and Margaret yelled from behind him,

"YOU FORGOT YOUR GOODY BAGS!"

She pushed Oliver out of the way and ran outside.

Oliver closed his mouth. Then he shut the door and locked it.

Later, when Oliver was in the bath, his dad said, "Margaret and I will walk you to school tomorrow, instead of Paul and his mom. Would you like that?"

Oliver opened his mouth and Mom said, "Yes! That's a great idea."

Oliver closed his mouth, shook his head, and stood up.

"You can't get out yet," said Dad. "I have to wash your hair."

Oliver opened his mouth and his dad poured water over his head.

He sat down and spit out the water.

The next morning, it was Oliver's first day of prekindergarten. Dad and Margaret walked him to school. Oliver was wearing his T-shirt with the red engine on the front.

On the way, they met Jasmine, her dad, and their dog, Brutus.

"Hi, Oliver," said Jasmine. "Would you like to pet Brutus?"

Oliver opened his mouth and Margaret said, "Oliver's afraid of dogs."

Oliver closed his mouth and put out his hand to Brutus. Brutus wagged his tail. Oliver opened his mouth and Brutus licked his lips shut.

"YUCK!"
said Margaret.

When he got to school, Oliver met his teacher, Mrs. Samra.

"Welcome, Oliver," she said. "I like your train shirt. There's a seat for you between Paul and Azim."

Oliver looked around.

Mrs. Samra said, "Let's choose an activity."

Paul chose the blocks and
Azim went to the sandbox.

Mrs. Samra looked at Oliver. "What would you like to do?"

Oliver opened his mouth and ... waited.

But there was no sound. The words were inside, but they were used to staying there.

Oliver closed his mouth.

Mrs. Samra looked at his T-shirt and asked,
"Would you like to play with our train set?"

Oliver opened his mouth and ... still nothing.
No Margaret, no Mom, no Dad to take over!

Mrs. Samra said, "So, you don't want to play
with our train set?"

Oliver opened his mouth and ... finally the words tumbled out!

I REALLY WANT TO PLAY WITH THE TRUCKS, INSTEAD!

"Well done!" said Mrs. Samra. "I like a student who isn't afraid to speak up!"

Oliver was very tired after his first day of school, so he was put to bed early.

Later, in the middle of the night, there was a noise downstairs ...

Dad tiptoed down slowly, with Mom and Margaret creeping behind.

They saw light coming from the open refrigerator door in the kitchen.

In the middle of the floor sat Oliver, with a bowl of spaghetti. There was sauce on his face and noodles in his hair.

Mom opened her mouth and Oliver said,

"I DID WANT MORE 'GHETTI!"

Mom closed her mouth and stared at Dad.

Dad opened his mouth and Oliver said,

"AND, I WANT TO WALK TO SCHOOL WITH PAUL AND HIS MOM!"

Dad closed his mouth and stared at Margaret.

Margaret opened her mouth and Oliver said,

"AND, I'M NOT 'FRAID OF DOGS!

I LOVE DOGS!"

Margaret closed her mouth and stared at her little brother.

Oliver looked up at them.

So, Oliver opened up and kept on talking ...